P9-DUI-540

THE CHICKEN SISTERS

BY LAURA NUMEROFF

PICTURES BY
SHARLEEN COLLICOTT

A LAURA GERINGER BOOK
An Imprint of HarperCollinsPublishers

Library of Congress Cataloging-in-Publication Data
Numeroff, Laura Joffe.
    The chicken sisters / by Laura Numeroff; illustrated by Sharleen Collicott.
        p.   cm.
    "A Laura Geringer book."
    Summary: The chicken sisters drive a troublesome wolf home to his mother with
their overwhelming eccentricities.
    ISBN 0-06-026679-1. — ISBN 0-06-026680-5 (lib. bdg.)
    [1. Chickens—Fiction.   2. Sisters—Fiction.]   I. Collicott, Sharleen, ill.   II. Title.
PZ7.N964Ch   1997   96-30297
[E]—dc20   CIP
                                                                                          AC

Typography by Christine Kettner
1   2   3   4   5   6   7   8   9   10
❖
First Edition

For my mother . . . with a whole bunch of love

—L. N.

Violet, Poppy, and Babs were sisters. Violet, the eldest, couldn't see very well but loved to bake. She had to squint to see the dial on the oven, so the sunny kitchen in their little yellow house was often filled with smoke.

"Boy, do I love to bake," she would say.

Poppy and Babs always ate Violet's cookies and cakes.

"Yummy," Poppy would say, delicately wrapping the burnt edges in her napkin.

"Scrumptious," said Babs, pecking gently past the parts that were burnt.

It made Violet happy to know her sisters liked her baking.

Poppy, the middle sister, loved to knit. She knit hats with chin straps, turtleneck sweaters with pom-poms, and covers for the lamps.

"Boy, do I love to knit," she would say.

She gave all the sweaters she made to Violet and Babs.

It made Poppy happy to know her sisters liked her knitting.

Babs, the youngest, couldn't hear very well, but she loved to sing.

She sang in the shower; she sang at Harriet's House of Hair, where she worked as a hairdresser. She even sang in bed.

"Boy, do I love to sing," she would say.

Babs sang off-key, but Poppy and Violet always applauded.

It made Babs happy to know her sisters liked her singing.

But the neighbors were not happy.

Bill and Tessie complained about the smoke. The Fontinis complained about the noise.

And the Fontini twins complained about the itchy wool hats Poppy gave them.

Whenever the neighbors played bridge, they discussed the sisters.

"There must be something we can do," Mrs. Fontini would say.

But they could never think of anything.

One day, an old wolf moved into the neighborhood. He couldn't wait to visit all of his new neighbors.

Bill and Tessie were so scared, they stopped going outside.

The Fontinis were scared too. When they went out, they disguised themselves in Halloween costumes. Mrs. Fontini dressed as a Martian. Mr. Fontini wore his old football uniform. And the twins went around dressed as salt and pepper shakers.

The old wolf was thrilled to see everyone so scared. He hadn't scared anyone in years. He crept up to Bill and Tessie's window and bared his false teeth.

He hid under the Fontinis' car and yelled, "Boo!"

The wolf liked the twins' costumes so much he wanted to dress up, too. He rummaged through his attic and found a deep-sea diver's suit, a mailman's uniform, and a ballerina's tutu. He liked the tutu the best.

Now it was time to visit the three chicken sisters.

He knocked on their door.
"Oh, a visitor!" Violet exclaimed. She invited the wolf in.

She offered him her freshly baked coconut crisps and he gobbled them down. They sat like rocks in his stomach. He stumbled over to the couch, moaning and coughing.

"Oh, my, you don't look well at all," said Poppy, pulling out a tape measure. "What you need is a nice sweater."

She measured his arms and chest. The wolf just lay there.

He closed his eyes.

At that very moment, Babs started to belt out her favorite song, "Puppies, Piglets, and Pumpkins, Too!"

"Doesn't she sing beautifully?" Poppy asked, still measuring.

The wolf tried to crawl to the door to get away, but he got tangled
in Poppy's knitting.

At that moment, Bill and Tessie and the whole Fontini family barged
into the house. They'd finally decided to complain about the singing
and the smoke. But when they saw the wolf, they froze.

"That's the mean old wolf!" gasped the Fontini twins.

"I'm not mean," the wolf cried. "I was just having fun."

"Fun? But you scared us!" said the twins.

"Please let me go!" the wolf pleaded. "I'll leave town. I'll even move in with my mother."

So the wolf went off to live with his mother in Atlantic City.

And the three sisters invited everyone to a party in their little
yellow house.

Violet made cakes and cookies. Babs sang. Poppy measured their heads for hats.

And their neighbors didn't complain at all.

The End